This book is dedicated to Claudia and Kate
(and long-suffering mums everywhere) ~ LP

LITTLE TIGER PRESS

An imprint of Magi Publications

1 The Coda Centre, 189 Munster Road,

London SW6 6AW

www.littletigerpress.com

First published in Great Britain 2008

Text and illustrations copyright © Liz Pichon 2008
Liz Pichon has asserted her right to be identified
as the author and illustrator of this work under the
Copyright, Designs and Patents Act, 1988

A CIP catalogue record for this book is available
from the British Library

Printed in Singapore

10 9 8 7 6 5 4 3 2 1

The Three Horrid Pigs

and the Big Friendly Wolf

Liz Pichon

LITTLE TIGER PRESS
London

Once upon a time, Mother Pig lived with her three horrid little pigs in a tiny house.

The little pigs were very naughty and they drove their mother crazy!

"I've had enough of you pesky pigs," she told them. "It's about time you moved out and found your own way in the world!"

So she packed their bags and sent them on their way.

Go on, clear off!

Stop pushing!

The first horrid little pig came across a big pile of straw. "This straw is PERFECT for me to build my house," he thought.

But the little pig was lazy. And he didn't make his straw house very strong at all. Luckily, a big friendly wolf (who just happened to be a builder) was passing by. "Good grief!" gasped the wolf. "What a mess that house is. I'll go and see if I can help."

"Little pig, little pig, may I come in?" asked the wolf. "PUSH OFF!" shouted the pig. "Not by the hairs on my chinny chin chin will I let a WOLF in!

Put one paw on my house

Oh dear!

and I'll **huff** and I'll **puff** and I'll

BOOT YOU OUT!"

"I only wanted to help," said the wolf sadly,
as he went on his way.

The second horrid little pig found a huge pile of twigs. "These twigs will make a brilliant house for me!" he thought. But the little pig was even lazier than his brother . . .

. . . so the house was a disaster!

When the friendly wolf saw the terrible tangle of twigs he thought, "Goodness me! That house is an accident waiting to happen. I'd better go and help!"

Goodness me!

"Little pig, little pig, may I come in?" asked the wolf.

"CLEAR OFF!" shouted the rude little pig. "Not by the hairs on my chinny chin chin will I let a WOLF in!"

and I'll **puff**...

and I'll

THROW

YOU

RIGHT

OUT!"

"I'm sorry," sighed
the wolf. "I only
wanted to help."

How rude!

The third horrid little pig was SO lazy, he couldn't be bothered to build a house at all! So he found a nice, cosy chicken shed instead . . . and moved in.

The friendly wolf just
happened to be passing.
"Oh my gosh!" he thought.
"Those poor chickens!
I must go and speak to that pig."

Pig's pinched
our house!

HELP!

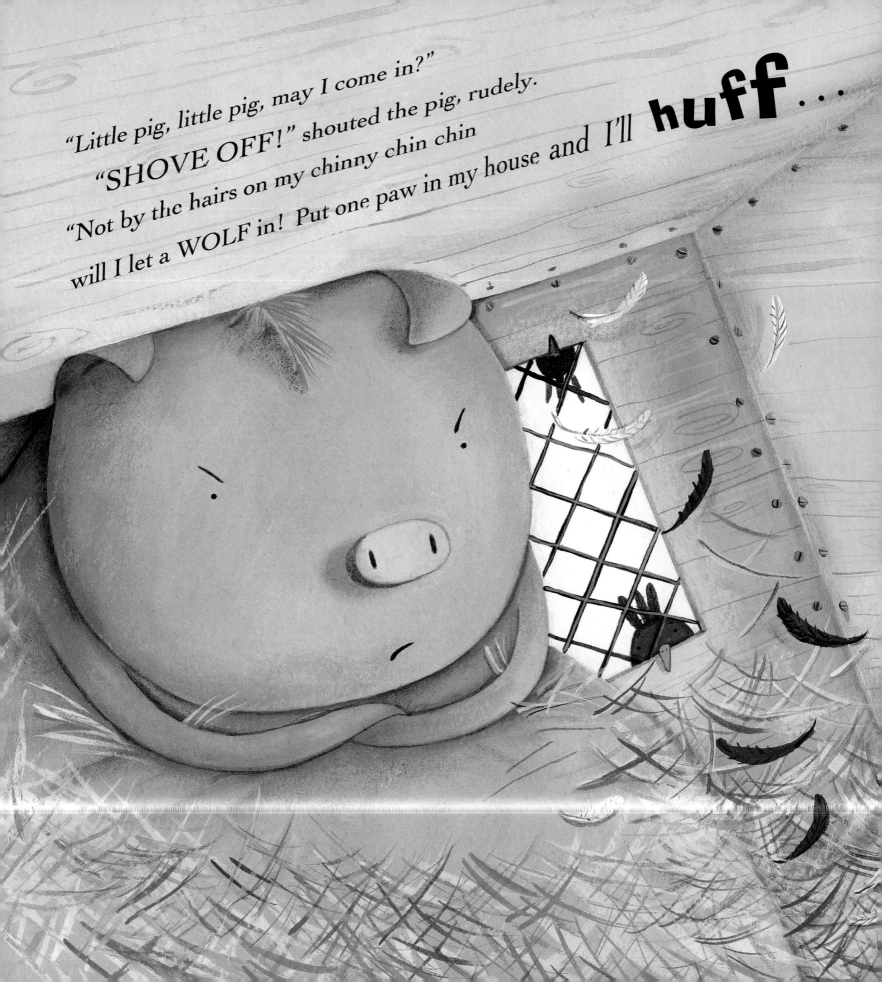

"Little pig, little pig, may I come in?"

"SHOVE OFF!" shouted the pig, rudely.

"Not by the hairs on my chinny chin chin will I let a WOLF in! Put one paw in my house and I'll **huff** . . .

and I'll **puff** and I'll . . ."

"Hold it right there!"
said the wolf. "This isn't YOUR
house. It's the chickens' house!"
"Who cares!" said the little pig.
"Now get lost, THE LOT OF YOU!"
What a horrid little pig he was.

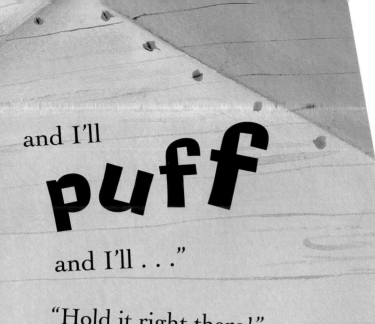

Charming!

So the kindly wolf invited all
the chickens back to HIS house,
which was built from bricks
and was very strong indeed.

WOLF'S HOUSE

Meanwhile, the house built
by the first horrid little pig . . .

. . . was being eaten up
by a herd of hungry cows.

The house built by the
second horrid little pig . . .

. . . was being pulled apart
by a flock of angry birds.

And the third horrid little pig . . .

*You've nicked
our TWIGS!*

Our NESTS!

. . . was being
pecked by a
cockerel, and went wee wee weeeeee eeeeee, all the way back
eeeeeeeeeee eeeeeeeeeeeeeee to his brothers
(which was *just* what
the cockerel wanted).

Now NONE of the pigs had a home. But the wolf did. And it looked very warm and cosy.

"This house would be perfect for us!" said the horrid little pigs.

So they waited until dark.
Then they climbed onto the roof
and began to slide down the chimney.
The wolf heard the horrid little pigs, so he got out a
GREAT, BIG POT OF BOILING ...

WOLF'S HOUSE

SOUP!

"You must be hungry!"
said the wolf.
He really was the
sweetest, loveliest wolf ever.

The End

The friendly wolf let the pigs stay.
And after a while they stopped
being lazy, horrid little pigs and
learned how to build a proper
house made of bricks . . .

. . . which was big
enough for EVERYONE!

And they all lived
happily ever after.